W9-BFN-569

Screaming Mummies of the Pharaoh's Tomb II

Tales from the House of Bunnicula Books by James Howe:

It Came from Beneath the Bed!
Invasion of the Mind Swappers from Asteriod 6!
Howie Monroe and the Doghouse of Doom
Screaming Mummies of the Pharaoh's Tomb II
Bud Barkin, Private Eye
The Odorous Adventures of Stinky Dog

Other Bunnicula Books by James Howe:

Bunnicula (with Deborah Howe)
Howliday Inn
The Celery Stalks at Midnight
Nighty-Nightmare
Return to Howliday Inn
Bunnicula Strikes Again!
Bunnicula's Pleasantly Perplexing Puzzles
Bunnicula's Long-Lasting-Laugh-Alouds
Bunnicula's Frightfully Fabulous Factoids
Bunnicula's Wickedly Wacky Word Games

James Howe is the author of the award-winning best-seller *Bunnicula* and its sequels, as well as many other popular books for young readers, including *The Misfits* and the Pinky and Rex series for younger readers. He lives in New York State.

TALES FROM THE HOUSE OF
BUNNICULA

Screaming Mummies of the Pharaoh's Tomb II

JAMES HOWE
ILLUSTRATED BY BRETT HELQUIST

Aladdin Paperbacks
NEW YORK LONDON TORONTO SYDNEY

First Aladdin Paperbacks edition January 2004

Text copyright © 2003 by James Howe
Illustrations copyright © 2003 by Brett Helquist

ALADDIN PAPERBACKS
An imprint of Simon & Schuster
Children's Publishing Division
1230 Avenue of the Americas
New York, NY 10020

Also available in an Atheneum Books for Young Readers hardcover edition.
Designed by Ann Bobco
The text of this book was set in Berkeley.
The illustrations were rendered in acrylics and oils.

Manufactured in the United States of America
10 9 8 7 6 5 4

The Library of Congress has cataloged the hardcover edition as follows:
Howe, James, 1946–
Screaming mummies of the Pharaoh's tomb II / James Howe; illustrated by Brett Helquist.
p. cm.—(Tales from the House of Bunnicula ; 4)
Summary: Howie the wirehaired dachshund and his friend Delilah collaborate on a novel, trying to win the coveted Newbony Award.
ISBN 0-689-83953-7 (hc.)
[1. Authorship—Fiction. 2. Dachshunds—Fiction. 3. Dogs—Fiction. 4. Humorous stories.]
I. Helquist, Brett, ill. II. Title.
PZ7.H83727 Hnr 2003
[Fic]—dc21 2002006669
ISBN-13: 978-0-689-83954-2 (Aladdin pbk.)
ISBN-10: 0-689-83954-5 (Aladdin pbk.)
1210 OFF

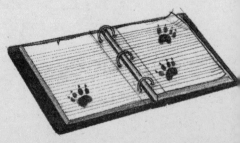

With thanks to Ginee Seo,
who is smart and funny
(not to mention as sensitive
as a finely tuned concert piano)

—J. H.

For Mary Jane

—B. H.

Screaming Mummies of the Pharaoh's Tomb II

HOWIE'S WRITING JOURNAL

I'm never going to write again!!!!!!!!!!!!

Uncle Harold, who is this really smart dog I live with who's written all these books about our rabbit, Bunnicula, who our cat, Chester (who is also really smart), says is a vampire because . . .

I forgot what I was trying to say.

Proof! I can't write! I'm never going to write again!!!!!!!!!!!!

1

Oh, now I remember.

Uncle Harold (who isn't really my uncle, I just call him that) says that he's gotten lots of bad reviews and that I shouldn't let one bad review get to me. Ha! Easy for him to say. He's been writing for a katrillion years and his books have sold a katrillion copies, even if he has gotten some stinko reviews. But I've written only three books. I've just gotten started. Nobody will want to read my books after what <u>Canine</u> <u>Quarterly</u>—my <u>former</u> favorite magazine in the whole world!!—had to say:

Howie Monroe writes with energy and a sense of humor, but he is a literary lightweight. Pack his books to while away the time when you're going for an extended stay at the kennel, but don't be looking for him to win the Newbony Award any time soon.

A literary lightweight!!!!!!!!!!!!!

Would a literary lightweight know how to use as many adjectives as I do? Or exclamation points!!!?

Oh, what's the use? If I'm never going to win the Newbony Award, why should I even bother to write?

I wonder what the Newbony Award is.

3

Howie's Writing Journal

My friend Delilah, who is this beautiful and <u>REALLY</u> <u>SMART</u> dog who lives down the street and happens to be one of my best friends in the whole world and is maybe even my girlfriend, although I've never told her that, not in so many words, anyway, well, Delilah said the Newbony Award is about the biggest award a book can be given. She said her owner, Amber Faye Gorbish, reads

Newbony books all the time. I told her Pete, who is Amber's boyfriend and one of the two boys who lives in the house with me (Toby is the other one), reads stuff like the Flesh-Crawler books by M. T. Graves. Those books are sooooooo cool. My favorite is #28: Screaming Mummies of the Pharaoh's Tomb. It's about these twins who find a time-travel machine in their grandfather's attic and ...

Anyway, Delilah said that books with titles like Screaming Mummies of the Pharaoh's Tomb never win the Newbony Award. I asked her what does win. She thought about it for a long time.

"Books that are sad," she said finally. "And take place a long time ago."

"Screaming Mummies of the Pharaoh's Tomb takes place a long time ago," I pointed out. "And it's sad. Especially the part where the screaming mummies crumble into about a katrillion pounds of dust."

Delilah gave me a look. "It also helps if the characters are poor and somebody dies," she went on. "Or if the main character, usually a child and preferably an orphan, goes on a long journey. Alone. Oh, and it should be a book girls will like."

A story started taking shape in my mind. (It's amazing how that happens when you're a writer.) I pictured a poor (but cute) dachshund puppy, without a penny or a parent to call his own, setting off in search of . . . something . . . and it's a long time ago, like last week, maybe, and . . . somebody dies.

I told Delilah.

"You need help," she said. "I've read a lot of Newbony books. Maybe we could write the book together."

I wasn't sure I liked that idea. I've never written with somebody else. Besides, I wanted

to win the Newbony <u>myself</u>. But then, I figured, half a Newbony is better than none.

"Okay," I said. "But can it still be about a
poor (but cute) puppy? And could he be
named Howie Monroe?"

Delilah didn't love that idea, but I reminded
her that I <u>am</u> a published author, so I should
get <u>some</u> say.

"Okay," she said, "as long as his friend—a
<u>girl</u> puppy named Delilah—has an important
part."

"Deal," I told her.

Newbony Award, here we come!!!!!!!!!!!!

Walk Two Bones

The Journey of a Poor (but Cute) Puppy Who Lived Long Ago (and Was Also an Orphan)

By Howie Monroe & Delilah Gorbish

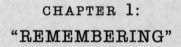

CHAPTER 1:
"REMEMBERING"

Howie Monroe, a lonely puppy who had no home, gazed sadly at his reflection in the pond. It was a hot summer day long ago when people (and puppies) were poor and the air was full of dust and yearning. Howie, seeing his haggard, ~~yet strong and incredibly handsome,~~ face, yearned for a chicken bone.

"That's all I ask," Howie said to no one but

the swirling dust and rippling water, "just a chicken bone with maybe a little meat on it to give me strength for my journey."

He thought back to how his journey had begun. It had been only days, yet it felt like years.

He had been happy once, but that was before the story started. Now he needed to be sad so whoever gave out the Newbony Award would take him seriously. He remembered frolicking with his brothers and sisters on the back forty behind the little house on the prairie where they lived with Ma and Pa Monroe and their sons, Peter and Tobias. Cows mooed contentedly about them, as lambs wobbled on their spindly legs.

"Be careful not to knock over any of the lambs wobbling on their spindly legs," Howie's mother advised him. She was wise and smart, just as Howie would grow up to be.

"I'll be careful, Mother," the sweet and affectionate Howie replied.

Howie rolled over in the clover, sniffing the sweet summer air. Suddenly he sniffed something that made him worry. Was it . . . could it be . . . ?

Yes! There was a change in the air. The cows stopped their mooing. The lambs stopped their wobbling. The puppies stopped their frolicking.

"Run!" Howie's mother cried out in alarm. "It's a tornado!"

~~Howie didn't have time to wonder where his father was. He figured he probably wasn't in the story at all, since most characters in Newbony books didn't have a father. Or a mother. Or both.~~

Ma and Pa Monroe were running toward them, desperate to save the animals who . . . whom . . . who . . . whom they loved as much as their own sons.

Howie~~, who was powerfully strong and whose little legs moved faster than the wind itself,~~ made it to the storm cellar just in time.

"Hurry!" he called to his family, but the door swung shut just as they reached it!

"Oh, no!" Howie cried out.

He was alone in the darkness. He sniffed around until his nose hit a strange object he had never seen before. As the storm raged above him, Howie asked himself, "What could this be?"

Suddenly it hit him!

~~It was a time machine!~~

HOWIE'S WRITING JOURNAL

Enough! I told Delilah she had to stop crossing out the good stuff I was writing, and she told me it wasn't good stuff and that was why she was crossing it out! Then I asked her where she'd come up with that dumb title of hers, and she said it was based on a fine literary novel that had won the Newbony Award one year and I said that was copying and she said my entire last

25

book (See Book 3: <u>Howie Monroe and the</u> <u>Doghouse of Doom</u>) was copying, and that's when we stopped speaking to each other and she went home.

I don't think I like this writing together business. I mean, who is she to cross out my writing and tell me she doesn't think a time machine has any place in a serious work of fiction!?

I asked Uncle Harold about it. He agreed that we were having a problem and that Delilah shouldn't just cross out what I've written without our talking about it, but he did think she was right to take out the adjectives I was using, especially since most of them were used to describe one particular character.

Uncle Harold has a real hang-up about adjectives. I think he's just jealous of how many I know.

But he did say, "You've got some impressive words in this chapter, Howie—'yearning,' 'haggard,' 'spindly.'"

I told him, "Delilah said we needed words like that in the story if we're going to be taken seriously."

"Well," he advised, "don't forget to make the story engaging. That's important, too."

I don't know what getting married has to do with writing. Sometimes I worry that Uncle Harold's mind is going.

Maybe what he means is that we have to make sure it's entertaining. Well, if there's one thing I know how to write, it's "entertaining."

I'm going to try writing the next chapter by myself. And while I'm at it, I'm going to change that dumb title of Delilah's.

The Terrible Secret
of the Pharaoh's Tomb!

By Howie Monroe & Delilah Gorbish

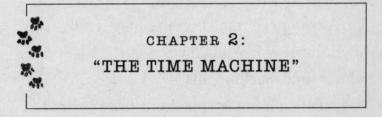

CHAPTER 2:

"THE TIME MACHINE"

"Awesome!" the enthusiastic and adventurous dachshund puppy exclaimed. "A time machine!"

He examined the machine closely. There was a dial with different settings in very small letters that read:

CAVEMAN TIMES

ANCIENT EGYPT

PIRATES

MEDIEVAL TIMES

THE WILD WEST

A WEEK AGO TUESDAY

"Awesome!" the bubbly and ready-for-anything Howie exclaimed. Again. "I wonder whose time machine this is."

Just then a boy stepped out from behind a barrel. It was Tobias, Ma and Pa Monroe's youngest son and Howie's favorite member of the family.

(NOTE to the real Monroes: *I like all of you!! This is a work of fiction!!*)

"Howie," Tobias said, "I think we'd better use this time machine to escape. I'm afraid the house is going to fall in on top of us."

20

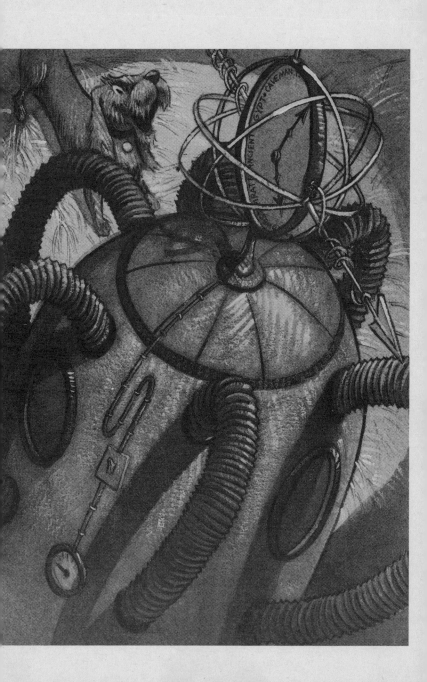

Howie didn't remind Tobias that they were in a storm cellar, which meant there wasn't a house on top of them, because he wanted to go in the time machine and have an adventure, even if it didn't win him a Newbony Award.

"Let's go!" he cried, although it came out as "Woof!"

"I've never actually used it," Tobias, who was sometimes called Toby, said. He picked up a book that was lying nearby. Its cover read, *How to Put Together Your Time Machine and Then How to Use It.*

"Hmm," said Toby, flipping the pages. "Oh, here it is—'Getting Started.'"

"Hurry!" Howie woofed as the sounds of the storm above them grew worse. The wind was howling. The cows were mooing. The dogs were barking. The lambs were baaaing. The trees were . . . well, you get the picture.

"I've got it!" Toby said, snapping his fingers. "We set the dial, get inside the capsule, close the hatches, and push the red button. I wonder where we should travel to. To where we should travel. To."

Anywhere but ancient Egypt, Howie thought. *I don't want to meet up with any of those screaming mummies!*

"Let's go to ancient Egypt!" Toby said.

"Nooooo!" Howie cried, but he was drowned out by crashing noises from outside and whimpering from nearby.

Howie and Toby turned to see a beautiful dog with bouncy blonde ears step out from under the stairs.

"I'm Delilah," the dog said. "I ran in here when I saw that a tornado was coming. I'm all alone in the world." A tear rolled down her snout. "Will you take me with you? Please?"

Toby looked at Howie. Howie looked at Toby. "What do you think?" Toby asked Howie.

The sympathetic, kind, and caring dachshund puppy had only one answer: "Hop in," he told Delilah.

It was only when the three of them were inside the capsule and the hatches had been closed that Howie remembered where they were heading: ancient Egypt!

HOWIE'S WRITING JOURNAL

Now, <u>that's</u> what I call writing!!!!!!!!!!!!

Delilah, of course, has a different opinion. "The whole thing is ridiculous!" she said. "You'll never win a Newbony Award with a story about going to ancient Egypt in a time machine. There's no depth, no character development! Let <u>me</u> write the next chapter!"

Ha! That's a laugh! As if she could write a chapter all by herself. Fine, let her try.

I told her she had to leave the story the way it was, though. She couldn't change anything, except maybe add some depth and character development. She didn't like that so much, but she agreed—as long as she could change the title. Titles are important, she told me, because they let the reader know the <u>tone</u> of the book. She said, "Don't you want the reader to <u>know</u> this is a Newbony Award winner and not something you pack up for a stay at the kennel?"

Well, that hurt.

"Fine," I said. "Change the title, but that's all!"

Delilah, Beautiful and Short

By Delilah Gorbish & Howie Monroe

CHAPTER 3:
"ACORN STEW"

Delilah had always been a good girl. She obeyed her parents, looked after her little brothers and sisters, and cooked for the whole family.

"No one makes acorn stew like Delilah," her granny had said in her final days.

It was the last thing Delilah remembered Granny saying, and a tear came to her eye

now, even as she was hurtling through time and space toward ancient Egypt. She had no desire to go there, really. It was a quirk of fate that had put her in a storm cellar with a strange boy and an even stranger dog as they were preparing to escape a tornado by traveling back in time.

Delilah sighed. Life had been a series of twists and turns for her. And losses, so many losses. But, no, she would not dwell on those, for she was not only a good girl, but a strong one.

She had been alone for a long time now. Weeks. She had had to live with her mean and miserly aunt Beulah Mae after the accident that had taken the lives of the rest of her family. There were days when she'd had nothing to eat but leaves and nothing to drink but rainwater. She had thought she might bring a ray of sunshine into her aunt's life, but Beulah Mae lived in the shadows of terrible secrets that haunted her from the past. Sometimes she would cry out in her sleep, keeping Delilah awake all night. It was too much to bear. Delilah set out on her own, with only the coat Mother Nature had given her on her back.

How long had it been since she had tasted acorn stew? Delilah shook the thought from her head. It didn't matter. What mattered was that she would have acorn stew again. Or would she? She would find happiness again. Or would she? She would not be alone. Or would she?

She comforted herself by softly humming

the lullaby her mother had sung to her as a puppy.

"What's that?" a voice asked.

Delilah woke from her reverie and stopped her humming. Howie, the strange dog sitting next to her in the time machine, looked at her with questioning eyes.

"It's the lullaby my mother used to sing to me," she said.

"My mother used to sing that same lullaby to me," said Howie.

Looking into each other's eyes, they began to hum the tune together. *Perhaps this trip to ancient Egypt wouldn't be so bad after all,* Delilah thought. Perhaps her days of being alone were over, and happiness was just a couple of millennia away.

HOWIE'S WRITING JOURNAL

BO-RING! Delilah calls that Newbony Award writing!? That's mushy girl stuff! Anyway, I was up in Toby's bedroom (Toby is a big reader) and I saw that he had lots of those books with Newbony Award stickers on them (they're so cool, they're shaped like a bone and everything) and I remember him reading some of those to me, and they were awesome books! I think Delilah's all wrong about what they have to be. I think there can be lots of adventure and good stuff. It doesn't have to be all sad.

I'm going to write the next chapter myself and show her.

And, oh yeah, I'd better point out to her that she didn't change just the title (even though she might be right about that). What's this business of putting her name <u>first</u> as author!?

Mummy's the Word!

A Serious and Sad (But EXCITING!) Mystery of Ancient Egypt

By Howie Monroe & Delilah Gorbish

CHAPTER 4:

"PHARAOH BEWARE-OH!"

Howie and Delilah stopped humming as the time machine hit the ground with a thud.

"We're here!" Toby cried, peering out of a window. "It's ancient Egypt!"

Howie was all ready to set his watch back to 2056 B.C. when he remembered he was a dog and didn't wear a watch.

"Let's go!" he yipped. Toby, getting the

message, threw open the door, and the three adventurers jumped to the ground.

What greeted their eyes was a parade of men in togas, women with these gold crowns on their heads that looked like snakes, and cats. Way too many cats.

"To the Egyptians, cats are sacred," Delilah pointed out.

"Another reason I knew we shouldn't have come here," Howie grumbled. But then he added brightly, "However, there are all the *Dogs* of Egypt."

"Dogs?" Delilah asked.

"You know, the Dogs the Egyptians worship in their temples, when they're not getting together at the Colosseum to watch gladiators fight to win the hand of Helen of Troy

and get a free ride in the big wooden horse."

"Oh, Howie," said Delilah, "you are so smart, not to mention wise and intelligent. How is it that you know so much?"

"I've read FleshCrawlers #28: *Screaming Mummies of the Pharaoh's Tomb*," the smart, wise, and intelligent Howie explained.

"Ahhh!" said Delilah. "Oooh!" She batted her eyelashes and tossed her curly blonde ears.

"Look out!" someone cried in ancient Egyptian.

Toby pulled Howie and Delilah off to the side of the road, which wasn't much of a road, since blacktop hadn't been invented yet.

A cat tore past them with something dangling from its mouth.

"Thief!" someone else cried. (In ancient Egyptian.) "Stop her! Yet do her no harm, since she is sacred, being a cat and all! Yet stop her anyway, for she has stolen the Amulet of Rah!"

"The Amulet of Rah!" Howie echoed. "What's an amulet?"

"An amulet," Delilah explained, "is a magic charm."

"Cool," said Howie, marveling that they had stumbled upon a mystery before they'd even had a chance to check into the Cairo Hilton and freshen up after their long trip. He also marveled at the fact that he was able to understand ancient Egyptian, but then, he *was* smart, wise, and intelligent, and besides, it was *his* story, so

HOWIE'S WRITING JOURNAL

Delilah tore the paper right out of my paws and said, "Who <u>says</u> this is <u>your</u> story? This is supposed to be <u>our</u> story, and Delilah is supposed to have an equal part!"

So now I'm waiting for her to finish the chapter.

Maybe I'll write my next book by myself.

Just a thought.

The Amber Amulet

By Delilah Gorbish & Howie Monroe

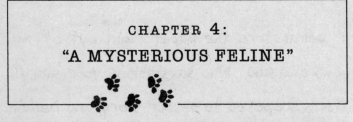

CHAPTER 4:
"A MYSTERIOUS FELINE"

Soon after they landed in ancient Egypt, Delilah and Howie became separated from Tobias.

"We're lost," Howie whimpered, "and there are cats everywhere!"

"Don't be afraid," said Delilah reassuringly. "I'm here to protect you. Besides, cats can't hurt us. We're dogs!"

"Like the Dogs of Egypt!" Howie exclaimed.

Delilah didn't know what Howie meant by this, but she felt it would be best to humor him, since he was not as bright as she and was also more easily scared. "Yes, Howie," she said in a soothing voice, "like the Dogs of Egypt."

Just then, a cat appeared, seemingly out of nowhere. She was walking with a limp and carrying a pouch in her mouth.

"Help me," she mewed piteously. "I am weak from hunger, but I must get this pouch into the hands of Princess Nefertiti before it is too late."

"But you can barely walk," Delilah said. The cat's condition tore at her heartstrings. "What is your name?" she asked kindly.

The cat answered in a voice that was barely

more than a whisper. "Rosetta. Rosetta Stone."

"That's a lovely name," said Delilah. Suddenly she was flooded with memories of the rose garden where she and her sisters used to play hide-and-seek. There, tucked among the rose bushes, was a large stone that was her favorite hiding spot. Surely, meeting someone named Rosetta Stone was a good omen.

"We'll help you," said Delilah.

"But we may be putting ourselves in danger," Howie objected, his body quivering with fear.

"I believe that Rosetta is on an important mission," Delilah told Howie in a no-nonsense manner. "We were sent from the twenty-first century to help her accomplish it. By doing so we will grow and mature in ways we couldn't have if we had stayed at home. It is only by going on our journey, by accepting the challenges that life gives us, by stepping up to the plate, by facing the dragon, by walking through the enchanted forest, by saying yes with our hearts when our minds tell us no, only then can we grow and change and be worthy of ~~the Newbony Award~~ all that we are meant to be."

Howie's tongue licked the tears that were rolling down his snout. "We were destined to be together, Delilah, two orphans traveling through time and space, enduring—"

"Whatever," said Delilah, "but first we have to help Rosetta here."

"Yes," Rosetta said, growing fainter by the minute. "Take this pouch to Princess Nefertiti. You will find her in the palace where she lives with her father, King Tut. She must have this before sundown or . . ."

Rosetta's voice faded away as her eyes rolled heavenward. The pouch slipped from her mouth and fell open. A tiny object rolled onto the sandy earth. It was an amber amulet.

"We must find Princess Nefertiti before sundown," Delilah told Howie, who was standing in a pool of his own tears. "Follow me."

Off they went in search of the palace of King Tut and his daughter Princess Nefertiti. Howie stayed close to Delilah's side, glancing nervously over his shoulder to see if they were being followed by cats. The only one he saw was Rosetta, and she was, well, dead.

Poor Howie, Delilah mused. *How he must have suffered in his life to be so afraid. I wonder what secrets lie hidden in his past.*

Once they were two strangers, but now the two puppies were bound together by fate . . . and an amber amulet.

HOWIE'S WRITING JOURNAL

Okay, there is <u>no</u> way I'm putting my name on this. I mean, I don't want to offend Delilah, but that last chapter is the worst thing I ever read. And doesn't she know the character of Howie would <u>never</u> stand in a pool of his own tears!? Not to mention the fact that he would <u>never</u> be scared all the time! Delilah keeps telling me I can't write girl characters—well, she's got a thing or two to learn about writing boy characters, that's for sure!

I'm in trouble. I'd better ask Uncle Harold for some advice.

HOWIE'S WRITING JOURNAL

Uncle Harold says the problem is that Delilah and I aren't <u>collaborating</u>, which means working <u>together</u>. He says we're fighting (no kidding) and we need to decide what we want to write and how we want to write it. He also said that we need to do some research because he was talking to Pop (that's Chester, the really smart cat we live with, remember?) and Pop said they didn't wear togas in ancient Egypt, that was ancient Rome, and a lot of other things don't exactly make sense either. Like the big wooden horse was from Greece and not Egypt. And the ancient Egyptians worshiped gods, not dogs. (If I'd had anything to do with it, they would have worshiped dogs!) And Nefertiti was King Tut's aunt or something, not his daughter, and he didn't think King Tut had any kids at all.

Picky, picky. Does anybody really care? I mean, this isn't a history book, it's literature! Besides, do Uncle Harold and Pop honestly think we have <u>time</u> to do <u>research</u>? Don't they know how many naps I have to take in the course of any given day? I hardly have enough time left over to <u>eat</u>, let alone write. Sheesh.

He probably thinks we should go back and <u>revise</u>. I hate that.

I'm going to leave everything the way it is. I mean, Pop <u>could</u> be wrong.

Besides, maybe my editor won't notice.

Howie's Writing Journal

    I talked to Delilah and we've decided that from now on we're writing this thing <u>together</u>. First, we have to come up with a title we can agree on.

Untitled

By Howie Monroe & Delilah Gorbish

CHAPTER 5:

"INSIDE THE PALACE"

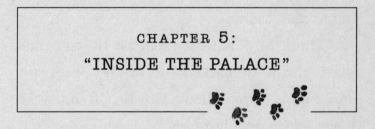

It did not take long for Howie and Delilah to find the Palace of King Tut. After all, this was 2056 B.C., so there weren't that many buildings.

The first person they met was a boy named Prince Papyrus. He told them that he was the son of King Tut, but that he and Princess Nefertiti had different mothers. "We have only Tut in common," he explained.

He seemed to know why they had come. "You have the Amulet of Rah," he said. "Follow me."

The palace was big, with many doors leading to many rooms.

"Think how hard it must be to keep this place clean," remarked the keenly observant and highly sympathetic Howie. "It must be loaded with dust bunnies."

"Dust bunnies!?" Delilah cried. "Did you say d-d-d-dust bunnies?" (See Book 1: *It Came from Beneath the Bed!*)

The strong and protective dachshund puppy was reassuring his frightened companion that he would not allow any dust bunnies to harm her when suddenly Delilah pushed Howie out of the way and

A door swung open and there stood

Princess Nefertiti. She was beautiful, but her beauty was only a mask for the deep well of sorrow within her.

"She is filled with tragedy, loneliness, and a longing for something that once was but can never be again," Delilah whispered, hearing echoes of her own life in the very words she uttered to describe another's. "I wonder what secrets she harbors."

Howie's eyes brimmed with tears. *He is so sensitive,* Delilah thought, *but then he has been wounded by life, and isn't it fair to say that all whom life has wounded are made either more sensitive or hardened to the point of not feeling anything at all?* How grateful Delilah was that Howie was the former, when he could so easily have been bored! Howie grabbed the pouch (and narrative) away from Delilah and dropped it (the pouch) at Princess Nefertiti's feet. He noticed that her toes were painted blue like the Nile, which he felt was a nice descriptive touch, then said, "Here's your pouch, gotta run." He was tempted to add, "After a while, crocodile," but thought better of it when he remembered he was in ancient Egypt and didn't know if crocodile references would be appreciated.

"Let's go," Howie said to Delilah, eager to get them out of the palace and off to someplace interesting. Like maybe the Pharaoh's Tomb, where there were sure to be some screaming mummies.

Howie's Writing Journal

So much for collaborating! Delilah went off in a huff and told me I could write the rest of my dumb book all by myself.

Fine.

I will.

<u>And</u> I'll give it the title <u>I</u> want it to have.

But first I'll take a nap. Collaborating is exhausting.

<u>Then</u> I'll give it the title I want <u>it</u> to have.

Screaming Mummies of the Pharaoh's Tomb!

By Howie Monroe & Delilah Gorbish

CHAPTER 6:
"THE CURSED CARTOUCHE"

Unfortunately the sun went down one minute before Howie and Delilah reached Princess Nefertiti. Too late for her! She keeled over and went into a deep sleep that would last for a hundred years, and would conveniently get her out of the way of the story, which was fine with Howie since he hadn't wanted her there in the first place.

"Which way to the Pharaoh's Tomb?" Howie asked Papyrus in ancient Egyptian. "My colleague and I are in search of the cartouche containing the secret of eternal life."

"Follow me," Papyrus answered, without giving any thought to the fact that a dog had just spoken to him in ancient Egyptian. After all, Egypt was the land of miracles and magic . . . and mystery!

The quick-thinking Howie nabbed the pouch that had been placed at the feet of the now horizontal (and snoring) princess. "You never know when an amber amulet will come in handy," he confided to Delilah, "especially when it is the Amulet of Rah."

"Oh, Howie," Delilah gushed, her left blonde ear cascading over her left eye, giving

her the look of a movie star or a one-eyed dog, "you think of everything."

"That's true," Howie said humbly.

Soon they were on their way. If Papyrus had not been there to guide them, it still would have been easy to find the Pharaoh's Tomb because there were so many signs.

One half mile to
the Pharaoh's Tomb

Pharaoh's Tomb Next Left

COMING SOON:
Britney Spears at the Pharaoh's Tomb!

When they were about two hundred camel's lengths away from the entrance to the tomb, Papyrus stopped. "I can go no farther," he announced in a voice shaking with fright. "Many have wasted their lives in the foolish pursuit of the cartouche containing the secret of eternal life. No one has ever found it. Most . . . have . . . never . . . returned!"

"Then we must turn back," Delilah implored, until Howie remembered he was supposed to let her be brave in this book.

"Let's go!" Delilah commanded.

"Fools!" Papyrus called out after them. "There is a curse on that cartouche! Go back to the twenty-first century where you belong!"

"Ignore him," Howie said to Delilah, which was easy enough to do until they got within twenty camel's lengths of the tomb entrance and heard the terrible sound coming from within.

"Screaming," Delilah said softly.

"Yes," said Howie. Could the sound be that of the fabled screaming mummies of the Pharaoh's Tomb? Could *they* be the guardians of the cursed cartouche?

What if what Papyrus had said was true? Would they never return? Howie heaved a deep sigh. What difference would it make if he *didn't* return? His family was gone. He was alone in the world. He had nothing to lose.

But if he were to find the cartouche of eternal life, he would have everything. The world would be his oyster, an expression he didn't understand but hoped his readers would.

"Are you with me?" he asked Delilah.

"The rancid breath of a thousand camels would not deter me," Delilah replied.

"My sentiments exactly," said Howie.

The two adventurers entered the Pharaoh's Tomb.

HOWIE'S WRITING JOURNAL

Oh, I'm good.

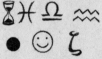

Everywhere they looked there was strange writing on the walls. Well it wasn't writing exactly, although it *was* strange. It looked sort of like this:

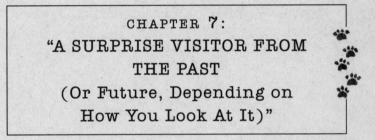

"It's too bad we don't have someone along who can read hieroglyphics," said Howie, who

had clearly done some research since Chapter 4.

"Ah, but you do, sir, indeed, sir, you do," said a small but familiar voice. What a surprise! It was Hoppy, the talking frog from Howie's last book. (See Book 3: *Howie Monroe and the Doghouse of Doom.*)

"How did you get here?" Howie asked.

"Anything is possible in fiction," Hoppy answered neatly.

"Cool," said Howie. "Can you tell us what these symbols mean?"

"Ah, that Hoppy can, sir," said Hoppy, putting on a pair of reading glasses as he balanced on Howie's head to get a closer look.

"Oh, dear," he said gloomily. "This is very bad, sir. Hoppy does not want to tell you what this says, sir."

"But you must," said Delilah. "We've traveled across time and space, without stopping at even *one* rest area named for a famous baseball player or local politician, to find the cartouche of eternal life. We can't let a few squiggly lines get in our way now!"

"Very well, miss," said Hoppy, hoping Delilah wouldn't get mad at him for calling her "miss" when he called Howie "sir." "It says, 'Not nice things will come on swift feet to whosoever dares enter this tomb and search for the cartouche of eternal life. In other words, if you know what's good for you, scram! And don't mess with the screaming mummies on your way out! You have been warned!'"

"Wow," Delilah said. "I wonder what the 'not nice things' are."

"Oh," said Hoppy, "it explains that. It says, 'The not nice things include, but are not limited to, snakes, spiders, scarab beetles . . . uh, dancing camels? (I think that may be a misspelling), and the aforementioned screaming mummies, who can really get nasty when their naps have been interrupted.'"

"Is that all?" Howie asked.

"Isn't that enough?" said Delilah.

"What about the smiley face?"

"Oh, that means, 'Have a nice day,'" Hoppy answered.

"That's sweet," Delilah said.

"Sweet, shmeet," the manly dachshund puppy harrumphed. "Let's go."

"And risk being trampled by dancing camels?" Delilah asked. "And letting loose upon the land beetles and spiders and snakes, oh, my, beetles and spiders and snakes, oh, my, beetles and—"

"Those are the chances we'll have to take," the brave and daring, not to mention courageous, Howie replied. "Now let's go get us a cartouche!"

"Oh, dear, Hoppy is frightened, sir," said Hoppy, but it came out, " Ω 〰 ."

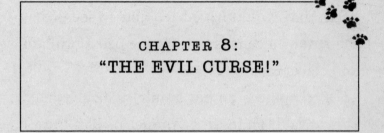

CHAPTER 8:
"THE EVIL CURSE!"

Hoppy led the way into the dark and creepy tomb. It was so dark they could not see a pin drop. Howie's eyesight, which normally was as sensitive as a finely tuned concert piano, failed him completely. No one had thought to bring a flashlight, since they had been in such a hurry to leave the twenty-first century, but a light bulb went off over the clever and brilliant wirehaired dachshund's head. (Note: This is just an expression. If a light bulb had really gone off over Howie's head, they would have been able to see. What the author means is that Howie had a brilliant and clever idea.)

"Perhaps the amber amulet will help us!" Howie said, taking the Amulet of Rah out of the pouch and holding it up.

Nothing.

"Say some magic words," the almost as brilliant and clever Delilah suggested.

"Abracadabra! Open sesame! Please and thank you!" Howie intoned.

The Amulet of Rah quivered in his hand. And then it began to glow with an amber light that grew brighter and brighter until they could see where they were standing.

"Awesome!" Howie breathed.

"Wow!" Delilah gasped.

"Hoppy is not happy," Hoppy whimpered.

They were surrounded by golden treasures and statues and little mummy cases with names on them like "Fluffy" and "Mittens."

"Let's start looking for the cartouche," Howie said, hoping that Delilah or Hoppy had a clue what a cartouche looked like. "Then we can go home and live forever, which will be nice as long as they don't run out of dog food."

"But where will we find it?" Delilah asked. "There's so much stuff in here. And it might not even be here. Look, there are three tunnels. Hoppy, what do those signs next to them say?"

Hoppy hopped onto Howie's head and read the signs by each of the tunnel entrances. "'Men.' 'Women.' 'Screaming Mummies.'"

"I pick door number three," said Howie.

Holding the Amulet of Rah in his mouth, he led the others through the tunnel marked "Screaming Mummies."

The room they came to at the end was even darker than the first room. The amber amulet barely lit up its interior, but the light was enough to make out a row of skeletons tangled in cobwebs.

"Oooh, gross," said Delilah.

"I thought the ancient Egyptians wrapped their dead and put them in mummy cases," said Howie.

"They did, sir," said Hoppy. "These are not

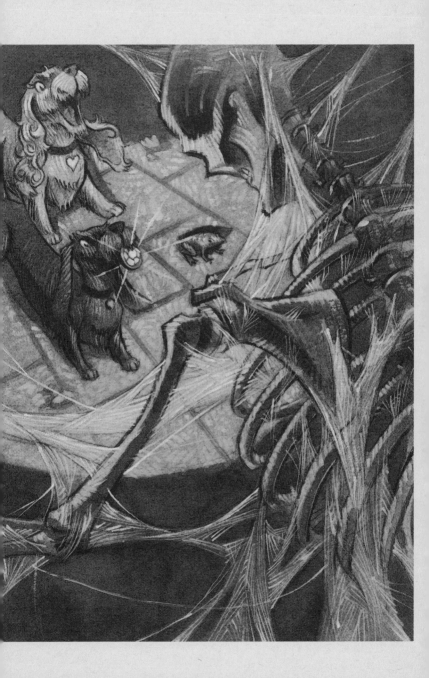

the skeletons of the ancient Egyptians. These are the skeletons of those who came before us. It appears, sir, that they did not, sir, find the cartouche of eternal life, sir."

"Good point," said Howie as the amber amulet began to fade.

"Nooooooo!" Delilah cried. Then, thinking quickly, she shouted, "Please and thank you! Open sesame! Abracadabra!"

The light began to glow, but something else happened too! Something really scary!

A big voice bellowed: "BEWARE THE EVIL CURSE!"

Before Howie could comment on the fact that whoever had spoken knew English—and uppercase English at that—there came a creaking sound, the kind you hear in movies when you know something really awful is about to happen, like a door is opening some-where and if the main characters were smart they'd turn tail as fast as they could, but they don't, they just stand there and all of a sudden you can't breathe and . . . well, it was one of those moments.

"Shine the amulet over there!" Delilah commanded.

Howie turned and pointed the amulet in the direction of the far wall, almost dropping it when he saw what was going on. Four mummy cases were opening (remember the creaking sound a couple of paragraphs back?) and now these really icky mummies with blotchy, stained shrouds stepped out and started screaming! Screaming so horribly that

Howie and Delilah and Hoppy could hardly stand it! They ran to the tunnel entrance, but it was gone! They were trapped, the amulet was fading, and they would never find the cartouche of eternal life at this rate!

"This way!" Howie yelled as the disgusting, foul-smelling mummies approached, their arms outstretched before them. But he quickly ran into the row of skeletons, becoming entwined in cobwebs. Delilah and Hoppy tumbled into him. There was no way out! It was all over! The mummies were getting closer with every step, screaming, screaming their horrible screams over and over and over!!!!!!!!!!!

Howie tried desperately to think what he could do to set them free. But what *could* he do? He was only one small dachshund in a world gone mad, one tiny voice in a sea of voices, one pebble in a field of boulders, one itsy-bitsy minnow in a school of sharks! He closed his eyes shut, wishing he was back on the prairie, romping with his brothers and sisters, wishing the tornado had never happened, wishing, wishing . . .

"Good morning, little puppy," he heard. "Time to wake up." Someone was licking his ears.

When Howie opened his eyes, he saw his mother's face.

"Did you have a bad dream?" she asked.

Howie looked around him. He was back at home, safe and sound. It had all been a dream.

THE END

HOWIE'S WRITING JOURNAL

Am I brilliant or what? I didn't know how to get the characters out of there, so I made the whole story a dream. I'll bet nobody's ever thought of <u>that</u> before! If that doesn't win me a Newbony Award, nothing will!

HOWIE'S WRITING JOURNAL

Great. I showed the book to Uncle Harold and he said, "Howie, having the whole story turn out to be a dream is a cop-out."

I didn't think Uncle Harold knew words like "cop-out." I guess he's still pretty cool, after all.

"But Uncle Harold," I said, "what am I going to do now? The story is a mess."

Uncle Harold agreed. He said the only way

out is to go back to Delilah and ask for her help, because the story is <u>ours</u>.

So that's what I did. (Oh, Uncle Harold also told me I can't use the title <u>Screaming Mummies of the Pharaoh's Tomb</u>, because M. T. Graves already used that title for FleshCrawlers #28. Who knew writing meant you had to be <u>original</u>?!)

Anyway, I went to Delilah and she agreed to help me out if she gets to write the last chapter all by herself. <u>And</u> give the book a title. Well, what I have to say to that is, "Harrumph!" But, hey, Delilah is half the reason the book is such a mess, so I may as well let her try to figure it out. Besides, the Monroes are out right now, which means I can sneak a nap on the sofa.

Life's Secret

By Delilah Gorbish & Howie Monroe

CHAPTER 9:

"GOING HOME"

The mummies' screaming wrapped Delilah
and Howie and Hoppy in its terrible sound,
much as the mummies themselves were
wrapped in linens. What the three adventurers
did not know was that the mummies were
wrapped in more than linens: They were
wrapped in the haunting secrets from their
dark and lonely pasts.

"Please don't be afraid," one of the mummies said as she tried to free Delilah, Howie, and Hoppy from the sticky spiders' webs. "We mean you no harm. We don't want to scream. We are cursed to do so because in our lives we were not kind to children and dogs."

"What about frogs?" Hoppy asked.

"Oh, we were especially not kind to frogs," said the mummy as the others nodded their agreement.

"We have learned the error of our ways, but it is too late for us. We are doomed to scream throughout eternity, but perhaps, just perhaps, we can yet do some good."

With a glance, Delilah indicated the skeletons at their feet.

"They were all frightened to death," said

the mummy. "You are the first we've had the chance to speak with."

"Give them the cartouche," said one of the others.

"Yes," chanted the third and fourth together. "Yes, yes, the cartouche, yes."

The first mummy handed the cartouche to the three adventurers.

"Is it cursed?" Delilah asked. "If we are granted eternal life, will it be as terrible as yours?"

"Oh, no," the mummy replied. "It does not contain the secret of eternal life, merely the secret of life. And the only curse is the curse of knowledge. Use it well, and your life will be blessed. Use it poorly, and you may end up like us."

Delilah opened the cartouche and asked Hoppy what it said.

"'The secret of life is enjoying the passage of time,'" Hoppy read.

"Oh," said Delilah, "thank you."

"Yes," Howie said, "your gift is a great one. I feel wiser and older and—"

"Hoppy is ready to go home now," Hoppy said.

With those words, who should they see at the entrance to the tunnel (which had miraculously reappeared) but Tobias?

"I knew I would find you here," Tobias said. "I have the time machine right outside the tomb. Shall we go?"

As they were leaving, Delilah turned back

and saw that the sound of the screaming mummies had changed to weeping. She wished she could make things different for them, but she understood that their fate was their fate, just as her fate was her fate, and Howie's fate was his fate, and everyone's fate was their fate, and so on and so forth.

"We can go home now and face whatever life brings us," Delilah said as she stepped into the time machine, "because we have traveled far, and we have learned much, and we have grown up."

"Fasten your seat belts," Tobias said as the hatch closed. "Next stop, the twenty-first century!"

Delilah smiled. Theirs had been a great and

noble journey, but all great and noble journeys must come to an end. Now it was time to sit back and enjoy the passage of time.

THE END

Howie's Writing Journal

Okay, not exactly the way I would have ended it. I mean, those screaming mummies turned out to be total wimps, but who knows, maybe Delilah's writing will help me win the Newbony Award. I'll tell you one thing, though. I am <u>not</u> sticking with that last title she came up with! <u>I'm</u> giving the book its title, and this is it:

SCREAMING MUMMIES OF THE PHARAOH'S TOMB II

I wonder if M. T. Graves will mind. I'm going to send him the manuscript and ask if it's okay to use the title. I mean, it's not <u>exactly</u> the same as his. Who knows? Maybe he'll even like my story! I mean, <u>our</u> story.

Afterword

What an honor it is to write a few words of praise for Howie Monroe and Delilah Gorbish's brilliant and innovative novel, *Screaming Mummies of the Pharaoh's Tomb II*. These daringly original (might I even say, cutting-edge) writers have done so much more than *extend* the story of my now classic work, Flesh-Crawlers #28: *Screaming Mummies of the Pharaoh's Tomb*. They have taken my meager crumbs and fashioned them into a feast! What depth and character development this book contains! Who could have dreamed that screaming mummies, so often portrayed as heartless villains (I myself am guilty of portraying them as such), could be reimagined as full characters haunted by their pasts? Yet does not the past play a part throughout this book, as if it were itself a character?

The hero's journey is of course an archetype of children's literature, but here it is given new form.

Indeed, "form" is given new form here, so that it is impossible for us to characterize this book as anything but what it is: *Screaming Mummies of the Pharaoh's Tomb II*. It is clear to me that Monroe and Gorbish are destined not only to exceed the 2.4 million copies sold of FleshCrawlers #28: *Screaming Mummies of the Pharaoh's Tomb,* but—dare I say it?— win themselves an award or two. I, for one, intend to dash a letter off to the Newbony Committee at once!

—M. T. Graves, author of the ~~166~~ 167
best-selling titles in the FleshCrawlers' series

What's next from Howie's overactive
imagination? Here's a sample from

Bud Barkin, Private Eye

By Howie Monroe

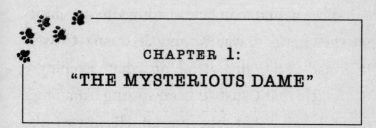

CHAPTER 1:
"THE MYSTERIOUS DAME"

I was working late. It was past my bedtime,
but I didn't care because twenty out of twenty-
four hours is my bedtime. I'm a dog. I'm a
detective. The name's Bud Barkin.

The light from the sign outside my window
was blinking like a firefly with a bad case of
the hiccups. I was used to it. The sign for the
Big Slice Pizzeria had been there as long as I

had. I'd just finished off a pepperoni and mushroom pizza—dinner alone, as usual—when I heard a knock on my door. My ears popped up like a couple of prairie dogs.

Who would come knocking on my door at this hour? I was hoping it wasn't Crusty Carmady. I'd just read in that evening's *Chronicle* that Crusty'd been sprung from Sing Sing. It was I that sent him up. His last words to me were, "I'll be gettin' outa here one of these days, Barkin. And when I do, put the water on fer tea 'cause I'll be payin' youse a little visit."

I inched my way across the room to the door. The top half of the door was frosted glass with words painted on it. A shadow fell across BUD BARKIN, PRIVATE EYE.

I held my breath.

"That you, Carmady?" I said.

There was the sound of breathing coming from the other side, but it wasn't Crusty's. I'd recognize his breathing anywhere. It was as raspy as a dull knife scraping across a piece of burnt toast. This breathing was fast and flighty, like a hummingbird with a bad case of the jitters.

I knew right away: The breather was a dame.

I pulled the door open. She toppled into me. One blonde curly ear hid half her face, but I could see right off she was Trouble with a capital T.

"Mr. Barkin," she pleaded, "you gotta help me."

"Do I, sweetheart?" I said. I may have been a private eye who was down on his luck, but I still had a way with words.

The dame was whimpering now. "C-Close the door," she stammered. "I'm being f-followed."

I did like she asked.

"Drink?" I offered, filling the extra water dish I keep handy.

"Don't mind if I do," she said, slurping as noisily as a gang of schoolkids splashing through a puddle at the tail end of a rainy day. I noticed that once she was inside the room, she didn't seem so scared. I smelled a rat and it wasn't pretty. This dame was up to something.

"What's your name, sweetheart?" I asked her.

"Delilah," she told me. "Delilah Gorbish."